The Berenstain Bears
and the
MAMA'S DAY
SURPRISE

Some mama bears are
so all-seeing and wise,
when Mother's Day comes
they're hard to surprise.

A First Time Book®

The Berenstain Bears
and the
MAMA'S DAY
SURPRISE

Stan & Jan Berenstain

Random House 🏠 New York

Copyright © 2004 by Berenstain Enterprises, Inc.
All rights reserved under International and Pan-American Copyright Conventions.
Published in the United States by Random House Children's Books, a division of Random House, Inc.,
New York, and simultaneously in Canada by Random House of Canada Limited, Toronto.
www.randomhouse.com/kids www.berenstainbears.com
Library of Congress Cataloging-in-Publication Data
Berenstain, Stan. The Berenstain Bears and the Mama's Day surprise / Stan and Jan Berenstain. — 1st ed.
p. cm. — (First time book) SUMMARY: As Mother's Day approaches, Papa Bear and the cubs do their
best to surprise Mama with breakfast in bed and a gift, and Mama does her best not to ruin the surprise.
ISBN 0-375-81132-X (trade) — ISBN 0-375-91132-4 (lib. bdg.)
[1. Mother's Day—Fiction. 2. Surprise—Fiction. 3. Bears—Fiction.]
I. Berenstain, Jan. II. Title.
PZ7.B4483 Beht 2004 [E]—dc21 2003000699
Printed in the United States of America First Edition 10 9 8 7 6 5 4 3 2 1
RANDOM HOUSE and colophon are registered trademarks of Random House, Inc.
FIRST TIME BOOKS and colophon are registered trademarks of Berenstain Enterprises, Inc.

Mother's Day was coming, and Mama Bear knew that Papa and the cubs were going to surprise her with a special celebration.

Last year they took her out for a special Mother's Day dinner.

Mama was pretty sure that this year they were going to surprise her with a special Mother's Day breakfast in bed. And alas, she also knew that she would probably have to spend the rest of Mother's Day cleaning up the mess they made preparing her special breakfast in bed. But that was okay. It's the thought that counts.

The signs of Papa and the cubs' Mother's Day plan weren't hard to read.

There was a marker in the cookbook at the page for Mama's favorite breakfast: Honeyed French Toast with Blueberries.

And one day when they were shopping at
the Beartown Mart, she saw the cubs slip off
in the direction of the card department.

As Mother's Day drew closer, Mama knew
that she had a lot to do if her family's Mother's
Day surprise was going to be a success.

First, she had to find the old bed tray they used when a family member was ill. She found it at the top of one of the kitchen cabinets where she kept jars and bottles that were too nice to throw away. It had some oatmeal on it from when Papa had been in bed with a cold. She scraped off the oatmeal and put the bed tray where she knew Papa and the cubs could find it.

But there was more to do. She had to make sure they would have the ingredients to make her special Mother's Day surprise. She checked the recipe in the cookbook. Honeyed French Toast with Blueberries called for honey, bread, eggs, sweet cream, sweet butter, powdered sugar, and blueberries. It was Papa and the cubs' favorite breakfast, too. But that was okay. It's the thought that counts. As for the mess they would make in the kitchen—well, that just came with being a mama.

Mama checked the cupboard. There was honey, of course, and plenty of bread.

There was powdered sugar, too. But it was all caked up like a rock.

They were out of eggs. But that wouldn't be a problem. She could get farm-fresh eggs from Farmer Ben. Nor would sweet cream, sweet butter, and powdered sugar be a problem. She would get those at the supermarket. But fresh blueberries? It was much too early in the season for blueberries.

The cubs were with Mama on her next trip to the supermarket. She didn't want to spoil their surprise, so she gave them a little shopping list to take care of while she put sweet cream, sweet butter, and powdered sugar into her cart.

She also bought some extra cleanser and scouring pads for the big Mother's Day clean-up.

She looked high and low for blueberries, but there were none to be found. It turned out that Gran had frozen some last season. That took care of the blueberries.

Mama was also pretty sure that a new bathrobe was going to be part of her Mother's Day surprise. She caught the cubs checking the size of her old threadbare one. But she pretended not to notice. As the big day drew closer, Mama made sure to stay out of the way when she thought they might be wrapping presents.

Finally it was the night before the morning of the big surprise. Papa and the cubs were doing their best not to let on that anything the least bit special was happening. But their secret smiles gave them away.

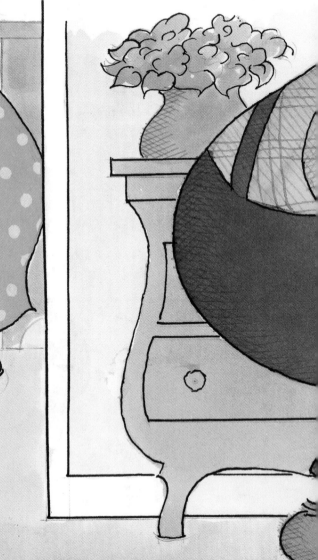

"Now, here's the plan," said Papa while Mama was off putting baby Honey Bear to bed. "I'm setting my wristwatch alarm for five o'clock in the morning. I'll set the alarm low so it won't wake Mama.

"Then I'll slip out of bed and come wake you two, and we'll sneak downstairs to the kitchen. Now, it's going to be very dark, so we'll have to be careful not to bump into things or we'll wake Mama."

Mama pretended to be asleep when
Papa's alarm went off. She lay perfectly
still as Papa slipped out of bed.

There was a certain amount of bumping and thumping as Papa and the cubs stumbled around in the dark. Papa even slipped and almost fell down the stairs, but the cubs caught him.

Mama lay awake getting ready to be surprised. But it wasn't easy. From the sound of it, things didn't seem to be going well down in the kitchen. The sound of an eggbeater was to be expected. But then there was a big clunk. What happened? Oh, dear. It wouldn't be the first time Papa dropped the bowl while he was beating eggs.

And what was that burnt smell? They must have burnt the toast.

Mama could just picture the mess they were making in the kitchen. It was all she could do to stay in bed. But after a few more clunks and some muffled shouts, she slipped out of bed, put on her old bathrobe, and stole downstairs to sneak a look at the kitchen.

It was the worst kitchen mess she had ever seen. The bowl had broken, so there was broken crockery and egg all over the floor. There was burnt toast on the drainboard and sticky honey handprints on the walls.

Oh, *dear*, thought Mama,
it's going to take me a week
to clean up the mess. Thank
goodness Mother's Day
comes just once a year.

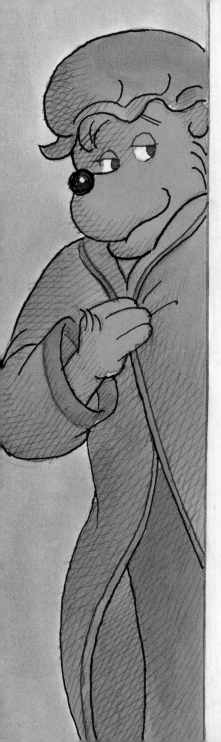

But out of the wreckage of broken crockery, spilled eggs, burnt toast, and sticky honey, Papa and the cubs had managed to put together a beautiful breakfast tray of Mama's favorites:

honeyed French toast with blueberries, sassafras tea, and even a small vase of red roses.

Mama sighed. It was so beautiful that it was almost worth the terrible mess they had made.

But now they were coming out of the kitchen and heading for the stairs. Mama had to get out of there or the whole surprise would be ruined. She scurried up the stairs and climbed back into bed.

She pretended to be just waking up when they came into the room with her breakfast tray.

"Happy Mother's Day!" said Brother and Sister.

"Happy Mother's Day, my dear," said Papa as he placed the tray on the bed and plumped the pillow behind Mama's back.

"Mother's Day?" said Mama. "Well, I suppose it is! How lovely! All my favorites: honeyed French toast with blueberries and sassafras tea and these beautiful roses. And look! Just what I needed!" she said as she unwrapped the new bathrobe.

"This is absolutely delicious!" said Mama as she ate her French toast and sipped her sassafras tea. "I don't know how to thank you."

Just then they heard baby Honey Bear's cry of "*Mama! Mama!*"

"I'd better get Honey Bear up and give her breakfast," said Mama.

"No," said Papa. "This is Mother's Day. You just stay in bed and read your cards. The cubs and I will take care of everything."

And they did.

When Mama got downstairs to go to work on the kitchen, she got a *real* surprise. It was the cleanest, shiniest, spick-and-spannest kitchen she had ever seen.

"Well," said Sister, "how did you like your Mama's Day surprise?"

"Yes," said Brother. "How did you like it?" Honey Bear gurgled and Papa beamed.

"How did I like it?" she said. "It was the most wonderful surprise any mama ever had!"

Then she gave her cubs
a great big Mama Bear hug.